Nana
IN THE
Country

BY LAUREN CASTILLO

CLARION BOOKS
An Imprint of HarperCollins Publishers

Clarion Books is an imprint of HarperCollins Publishers. | Nana in the Country | Copyright © 2024 by Lauren Castillo | All rights reserved. Manufactured in Italy. No part of this book may be used or reproduced in any manner whatsoever without written permission except in the case of brief quotations embodied in critical articles and reviews. For information address HarperCollins Children's Books, a division of HarperCollins Publishers, 195 Broadway, New York, NY 10007. | www.harpercollinschildrens.com | Library of Congress Control Number: 2023937522 | ISBN 978-0-54-410217-0 | The artist used ink, watercolor, and pastels to create the illustrations for this book. | Design by Whitney Leader-Picone
23 24 25 26 27 RTLO 10 9 8 7 6 5 4 3 2 1 | First Edition

In memory of my nannie,
and for nanas and grandchildren
everywhere

Nana came to stay with me in the country.

I've missed my city nana,

and I can't wait to show her everything I love.

The country is friendly.

I thought Nana would be nervous.
But she's not shy at all.

The country is wild.

It has all kinds of crawly creatures.
But Nana isn't scared.

The country is filled with magical things.

But Nana doesn't seem surprised.
Not even a bit!

I can't show Nana how to do anything in the country.

She already knows how to do it all.

Before bed, we have to tuck in the animals.

First the chickens.

Then the sheep.

I climb under the covers,
and we say good night.

"I can't wait to learn more about the country
tomorrow," Nana says.

Suddenly a loud thunderclap shakes the house awake.

"The sheep!" Nana cries. "It's loose!"
Nana is scared, but I remember a trick.

I grab a treat

and rush outside.

Step . . .

. . . by step,

I herd the sheep right back to its pen.

Nana claps.

Before long the sun comes up, and it's time for chores.

I show Nana how to give the animals fresh water.

I feed the chickens by myself and show
Nana where to find the eggs.

She is impressed.

Nana says the country is friendly.

She says it's wild.

She says it's filled with the most magical thing—ME!

When it's time for Nana to leave,
I tuck a souvenir into her city hat.

The country is friendly, the country is wild,
and the country can't wait for
Nana to visit again soon.